천 개의 햇살
여기 그대 곁에

I am a thousand sunbeams, here beside you

여기 그대 곁에

펴낸곳 (주)도어스
지은이 강영희
그린이 이성표
디자인 조의환
펴낸이 김동규
초판1쇄 2017년 9월 23일
주소 03169 서울 종로구 사직로10길 7(내자동)
전화 070-4231-4232
Facebook 강영희
Twitter @gumunjadab
Instagram kang_younghee_love
홈페이지 9moon.co.kr
등록번호 2016년 5월 12일 제300-2016-54호
ISBN 979-11-958208-6-3
값 13,000원

천 개의 햇살
여기 그대 곁에
I am a thousand sunbeams, here beside you

강영희 글 | 이성표 그림

번역 Translation

Mi Na Sketchley

Korean Translator & Conference Interpreter

MA MCIL DPSI Korean (English Law) NRPSI

Reading for DPhil Oriental Studies, Oriental Studies

Faculty, University of Oxford

Anthony Charles E. Banks

Editor and proofreader. ESL professional

University of London

Hyangkue Lee

Independent Researcher, Writer and Translator

PhD. Education, Seoul National University

차례 Contents

호랑이가 나타났어

The Tiger is Back in Sight

호랑이가 나타났어

The tiger is back in sight

1-1

어흥 호랑이가 나타나 옛날 이야기를 시작했어

호랑이 담배 먹던 시절엔 말야 화롯불 가운데 놓고 정답게 지냈거든

화등잔 호랑이 눈에서 닭똥 눈물 떨어졌어

가슴 복판에 커다란 구멍 뚫려 버렸어

바보 같은 호랑이가 무슨 짓을 한 거야

Roar, the tiger has turned up and started an old tale

"Many moons ago, when the tiger used to puff away,

everything was so cordial around the brazier."

The tiger's flame-filled eyes shed large tear drops

A huge hole is now bored right in the middle of my heart

Silly tiger – what have you just done to me?

A Chartreuse bird is flying in the air

The bird comes into the house and I shut the window with my trembling hands

Jumping and leaping, the bird dances

She then falls and pukes up her cherry red coloured blood

I slip away to open the window

The bird soars into the air, out the window

Spring birds are flying through the immensity of the world: Chirp Chirp

연두빛 새 한 마리 하늘을 날은다

새는 어느새 집안으로 들오고 떨리는 손으로 창문을 닫는다

새는 펄쩍펄쩍 춤추고 춤추다 쓰러져

앵두빛 피를 토하고

나는 어느새 창문을 열은다

창문 밖으로 휘릿쫑 새가 날으고

천지에 봄 새가 날아 봄봄

호랑이가 나타났어
The tiger is back in sight

1-3

A well-bucket is coming down from the sky

Is it a gift from an angel?

I embrace the bucket with my fluttering heart

The bucket is filled with pristine air

My body shrinks under this false hope

I shall be with you

As a clean and clear gift from an angel, I shall be with you

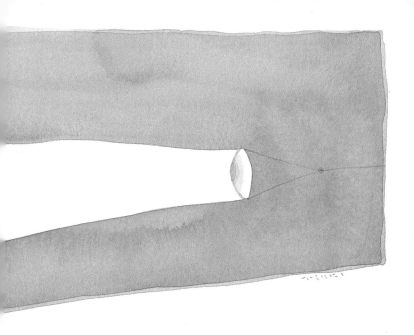

하늘에서 두레박이 내려와요

선녀님이 보내신 선물일까요

설레는 마음에 두레박을 안아요

빈 두레박 속에 맑은 허공 들었네요

허황한 마음에 몸이 자꾸 작아요

이제 당신께 갈래요

선녀님이 보내신 맑고 맑은 선물되어 당신 품으로 갈래요

황소 한 마리 어두운 겨울 들판에서 울부짖고 있었어

마음 속의 집착을 버려야 봄이 온다고 했지

내가 사라져야 사랑이 시작된다고 했어

봄이 올 수 있을까

종달새 우짖는 봄이 오려면 마음 속의 황소 한 마리

조용히 나동그라져야 할 텐데

An ox was lowing in the gloomy winter field

She said I must dispel the clinginess in me if I want Spring to arrive

She said I must disappear if I want love to start

Would Spring be coming?

To have Spring full of larks' carols,

the ox in my heart ought to be quietly discarded.

어쩔 줄 몰라요 당신이 좋아서

그러다 잡은 손 슬며시 놓아요

깜짝 놀라 당신을 찾지만 그 모습 보이지 않아요

허둥허둥 빈 손 저으니 뜨거운 눈물 몸 속을 흘러요

손 놓고 어느새 가슴으로 오신 당신

어쩔 줄 몰라요 당신이 좋아서

My fondness for you makes me giddy with joy

But then our clasped hands are loosened stealthily

I look for you in consternation but you are nowhere to be seen

While my empty hands are floundering, burning tears are flowing down into me

My dear, you slipped into my heart after letting go of our hold

My fondness for you makes me giddy with joy

쌀이 붇고 물이 끓고 뜸도 들어야 해요 밥을 지어주는 시간들이 고맙다구요

하지만 그건 우리들의 시간이에요

귀한 시간 기다림으로 덜어내어 우리를 공양하는 빈 마음보다

값진 것은 없을 거예요

말없이 밥솥 바라며 기다림을 배워요

It takes time for rice to be soaked in water, boiled and steamed thoroughly

Are you saying you are thankful for the time we take?

But the time is for us

There is nothing richer than your empty mind which makes an offering to us

by taking its precious time

I learn what 'waiting' is, since I am facing the rice cooker

몸뚱이 따위 없어도 좋아
새끼 발가락 만큼 작은 몸뚱이에 슬쩍 마음 붙이고 살아도 좋을 거야
갈수록 작아지다가 옷 한 벌 벗어놓고 사라져도 좋을 텐데
두리번 날 찾다가 아하 고개 끄덕이며 하늘 쳐다보는
당신 보는 것도 괜찮을 거야

I don't even need a body
I wouldn't mind if my body were as tiny as a little toe as long as
my heart is there
I don't mind if my body shrinks bit by bit and finally vanishes,
with just a pile of clothes remaining
Searching for me, looking up at the sky, with a nod of your head,
you will say "Aha!"
I wouldn't mind at all, just to gaze down at you.

I tried to run away desperately from a python I met but she followed me
to the end

I turned into a woman muffled up under the python's skin

Then, here comes Spring

With an overwhelming surge, I killed the python with a single stroke

You see, to put on the heat-hazed spring duvet, one needs to be
mother-naked with viridity

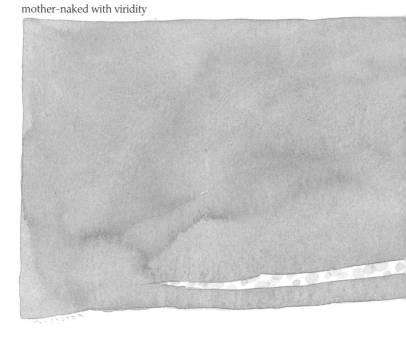

구렁이를 만났어 기를 쓰고 도망쳤지만 끝까지 따라왔어
구렁이 껍질을 뒤집어쓴 구렁이 여자가 되었어
그런데 봄이 오시는 거야
복받치는 마음에 단칼로 구렁이를 죽였어
아지랑이 봄이불을 덮으려면 싱그러운 알몸이 되어야 하잖아

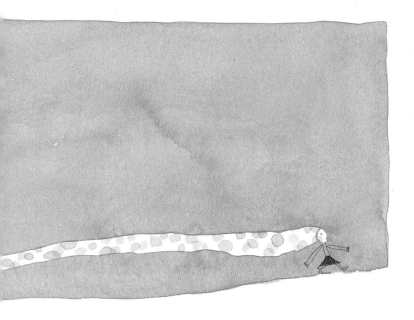

기차는 떠나네

The Train is Leaving

The train is leaving at 7

The train is leaving as it nurtures Nidana of people in each coach,

standing like bean sprouts, curving through the cloudy sky

Turning away from the last coach as I fail to find you even there

There I see you, beams of sunlight, cutting through the murky sky, joining me

The train is leaving, just like that

기차는 7시에 떠나네

칸마다 콩나물 인연들 기르고 부연 하늘 가르며 기차는 떠나네

마지막 칸에도 당신 얼골 보이지 않아 덜컹 뒤돌아보며 떠나는데

뿌연 하늘 가르는 햇살되어 함께 가시는 당신

그렇게 기차는 떠나네

꽃 한송이 입 속에서 피어나요

입 다물어도 입이 벌어져요

와글와글 꽃말이 들려와요 세상의 꽃

여러분 안녕하세요 사랑 없는 세상이 왔답니다

수근수근 꽃말이 들려와요

어서들 꽃을 피웁시다 사랑 없는 세상에서 안녕할 수 없답니다

A flower is blooming inside of my mouth

It gapes even when I try to close it

Babble babble, I hear the flowers' words

"Hello all my honoured flowers, the world without love has come."

Murmur murmur, I hear the flowers' words

"Let's hurry up and bloom. We can't be safe in the world where

there is no love"

봄봄 봄이 와요

골목길 주황 쓰레기통 노랑 길냥이 부연 털에도 얼룩덜룩 봄이 와요

슬며시 손 내밀어 손바닥에 담아요

주먹에 든 봄을 하낫둘 세어요

아직도 졸고 있는 어린 길냥이 기지개 켤 때까지 살며시

봄봄 가만가만 봄봄

Bom Bom - Spring is coming

onto the orange bin down in the alley, onto the gingery hair of a street kitten,

a variegated Spring is coming

I stretched out and put Spring in my palm

I count Spring in my fist - one, two

Until the sleepy little kitten stretches after a sound sleep

Bom Bom, softly gently, *Bom Bom*

Bom
Bom is transliteration of a Korean word (봄), the equivalent of 'Spring'.

길다란 지팡이 짚고 꼬부라진 할머니가 나타났어

소매 끝 붙잡고 할머니를 졸라댔지

할머니 할머니 사랑 이야기 들려주어요

사랑 타령이 나오자 할머니는 호물호물 사라졌고

길다란 지팡이가 꼬부랑 사랑 이야기 늘어놓았어

A bent over old woman appeared with a long walking stick

Tugging on to her sleeve, I begged her

"Please tell me your love story"

As the nagging of love pops up, the old woman vanished into thin air

Then the long walking stick started to unravel the twisted love story

기차는 떠나네

The train is leaving

2-5

I saw a tree on a snowy day

The bare tree looked like a naked man and

the big fluffy snowflakes looked like a bride in a white dress

All of a sudden, the man and woman became one and the white snow flowers

bloomed on the tree

I was puzzled by this love play enacted by Heaven and Earth

The world was full of love

눈오는 날 나무를 보았어요

헐벗은 나무는 벌거벗은 남자로 보였어요

굵어진 눈송이는 소복 입은 신부로 보였구요

순식간에 남자와 여자가 하나되었고 나무 위에 하얀 눈꽃 열렸어요

천지의 사랑놀음에 어안이 벙벙해요

세상은 온통 사랑이더군요

사랑에 빠졌다고 했더니 모두들 물었어
얼굴이 예뻐요 돈이 많아요 바보처럼 착해요
하는 수 없이 백지를 내밀었어
당신이 곁에서 수줍게 말했지 냄새가 난다고 했잖아요
백지에 코를 대고 냄새를 맡았어 코를 맞대고 한바탕 웃었지

When I said that I had fallen in love, everyone asked,

"Is she pretty, is she wealthy, is she foolishly good-natured?"

The only way I could answer was to thrust a blank piece of paper at them

You, sitting next to me, said bashfully

"You told me that it held a scent"

We smelt it together nose to nose, and burst out laughing

가슴이 내려앉았어

당신이 너무 아름다웠거든 나도 몰래 헐벗은 가슴 드러내었어

당신이 너무 위태로웠거든

가슴에 당신을 품고 정신없이 달렸어

달리다 떨어져 산산조각 나려는데 아름다운 손이 불쑥 구하시는 거야

아름다운 당신 때문이었겠지

Your staggering beauty made my whole heart sink

How precarious you looked, I exposed my naked chest

without even thinking about it

I held you in my arms and dashed at full speed

At the very moment when I was so close to falling apart,

an alluring hand suddenly saved me

Perhaps it's all because you are so very alluring

I have a confession to make

I died suddenly without having a clue about love

As a dead soul, I sensed a dim redolence - how bizarre

So here I am, confessing my love to you

I still don't know what love is but I love you as a very faint scent

고백할 게 있어요

사랑이 뭔지 아무것도 몰랐어요 그렇게 갑자기 죽었어요

죽고 나니 정말로 이상해요 아득한 향기가 느껴지는 거예요

그래서 이렇게 고백하고 있어요

사랑이 뭔지 아직도 모르지만 아득한 향기되어 당신을 사랑해요

A little child is coming down from the sky

Even a slightest hesitation would let go of the universe so I grab the child at once

The Sun rises, the Moon rises and the universe goes round and round

I keep pulling the child up

My worries pile up like a huge mountain but I can't help it

Because the only real love is reckless love

하늘에서 아이가 내려와요

덥석 아이를 안아요 잠시라도 망설이면 우주를 놓칠 테니까요

해뜨고 달뜨고 빙글빙글 우주가 돌아요

품에 든 아이를 자꾸만 추슬러요

걱정이 태산이지만 어쩔 수 없어요

유일한 사랑은 무모한 사랑이잖아요

A dazzling flower burst into bloom effulgently

As the flower is about to end her life with that dazzling delight,

an ugly lump – not even a flower – clenches on to the end of my sleeve

I end my life in sorrow just like this

"I am happy since I have loved"

With that final word behind her, she falls off from the futility of life

아름다운 꽃이 찬란하게 피었어요

그렇게 기쁨으로 한 세상 끝내려는데 꽃도 아닌 못생긴 덩어리가

소매끝을 잡아요

이렇게 슬픔으로 한 세상 끝내고 말아요

사랑하였으므로 행복하였네라

마지막 한 마디 남기고 허무하게 지고 말아요

Your love, the love which holds me firmly with your whole body,

the love which holds me when I lose my footing on a thousand-foot-high cliff

Our wings sprout out through your love and we flip over the cliff faraway

All the thankful days we pass by

Oh, what a sparkling life we have, so much like a pilgrim of love

하루가 끝나고 다시 하루가 시작되는 천길 낭떠러지에서
허공에 발딛는 나를 온몸으로 잡아주시는 당신의 사랑
사랑으로 날개를 달아 아득한 낭떠러지를 파득이며 건너가는
감사의 날들
사랑의 순례자 같은 우리들의 기쁜 생애여

거울 앞에 서는 것은 부끄러우나 당신 앞에 서는 것은 그렇지 않다네
너무 맑아 티끌마저 보이는 당신 앞에 서면 차라리 마음이 놓인다네
부끄러움 마저 잊고 당신의 맑은 얼골 넋놓고 바라본다네
풍덩 거울 속으로 몸놓고 사라진다네

I am rather embarrassed when standing in front of a mirror but not before you

When I face you, your face is so very clear even a speck can be spotted,

I am rather relieved

I even forget the sense of shame and gawk at your crystal-like face

Splash, I fade away into the mirror, leaving my body behind

당신이 좋아

주름살이 늘어도 당신이 좋아

별것도 아닌데 띌듯이 좋아

티끌이 보여 홉뜬 눈으로 보아도

어쩔 수 없이 당신이 좋아 하나에서 열까지

열에서 별까지

정말 좋아

당신 생각에 달콤한 솜사탕 마냥 조금씩 녹아내려요

I fancy you

I fancy you even when you are covered with more wrinkles

There is nothing special about it but I am full of delight

I fancy you even when I glare at you for a speck I spot

I fancy you from one to ten

from ten to the stars

I really do fancy you

Thinking of you, I melt bit by bit just like candy floss

어디서 무엇이 되어 다시 만나랴

Where and as What will We Meet Again

Where and as what will we meet again?

Will we meet again as a flowing river?

Will we meet again as a crying migrating bird?

Will we meet again as a choked-up grass bug?

I know you and I will meet again as something of beauty

Where and as what will we meet again?

우리 어디서 무엇이 되어 다시 만나랴

흐르는 강물되어 다시 만나랴

울어 예는 철새되어 다시 만나랴

목이 메는 풀벌레되어 다시 만나랴

너와 나 아름다운 무엇으로 다시 만날 것을 믿으니

우리 어디서 무엇이 되어 다시 만나랴

오래 기다렸어요

세상이 생겨나기 전 내가 작은 알이었을 때 그때부터 당신을 기다렸어요

작은 손 휘저어 알을 깨고 태어날 때 그때도 당신을 기다렸어요

여전히 기다려요 깨어나지 않은 사랑으로 내 안에 계신 당신

기쁨으로 당신을 기다려요

It has been a long waiting

I have been waiting for you even before the world was born,

even from when I was just a tiny egg

I have been waiting for you even from the moment when I was hatching forth

with my wiggly little hands

I am still waiting, waiting for you while you are resting in me as an un-awoken love

I am waiting for you with pleasure

산이 울고 강이 울었다 큰소리로 쩌러렁 울었다

울만큼 울고 패앵 코풀고 나서 까무룩 잠들었다

우리도 그랬으면 좋겠다 멋적은 웃음 나올 만큼 실컷 울고 나서

그네들처럼 잠들고 싶다

산이랑 강이랑 발뻗고 누워 나란히 뒹굴고 싶다

The mountain cried and so did the river, they howled loudly

After enough crying, they were worn out, blew their noses and drifted away

I wish we could fall into a sleep just like them after having enough of crying

which ends up making us laugh sheepishly

I just want to stretch out my legs, lie down and roll about next to the mountain

and the river

갑자기 뻥하고 귀가 뚫렸어

순식간에 펑하고 가슴이 뚫렸어

털썩 주저앉아 엉엉 울었어

아름다운 봄이 앞에 있더군

울지마

날 사랑한다는 너의 소리가 천지를 울렸어

그래서 이렇게 먼 길을 물어물어 왔잖아

그리운 봄이 앞에 있더군

All of a sudden, my ear popped

In a fleeting moment, my heart popped

I plopped down and wept loudly

Brilliant Spring was standing right before me

"Don't cry my dear."

Your voice flared out over the entire Earth

"That's why I asked here and there through all that journey to find you."

The longing Spring was right in front me.

흐르는 것이 물 뿐이랴

저물어가는 시간의 강물에 마음을 씻고 이제 풍요로운 잔치상 놓인

그리운 마을로 돌아가야 한다

흐르는 물 따라 가난한 시간 흘러가는 걸 보았으니

우리들의 가난도 흐르는 시간 따라 흘러가는 걸 보았으니

It's surely not just water that flows

We shall wash down our hearts in that river of time and return to the longing village

where a hearty feast is laid out

Because we saw the time of need flowing away along the water

Because we saw our poverty drifting away along the flow of time

I exclaimed to the sky

"Thank you for sending my love to me."

The sky shouted back

"Thank you for sending my love to me."

Lol Lol

The sky must be a copycat

That's what I had shouted!

The sky shouted back in silence

"Thank you for sending my love to me."

Boo hoo

The sky must be a copycat

하늘을 향해 외쳤어요

이 사람을 보내주셔서 고마워요

하늘이 큰 소리로 외쳤어요

이 사람을 보내주셔서 고마워요

깔깔

하늘은 따라쟁이인가봐

그건 내가 한 말이잖아요

하늘이 말없이 외쳤어요

이 사람을 보내주셔서 고마워요

엉엉

하늘은 따라쟁이인가봐

Samshin Granny's

In the traditional beliefs of Korean, Shamshin Granny is a goddess who blesses unborn babies and protects their mothers with a safe delivery. Shamshin Granny represents the generous embracement of Mother Earth which bears and rears life. She is often illustrated as a goddess who lives in *Anbang* (in the master bedroom) at peoples' houses.

큰 솜이불 지어 지구를 포옥 덮어주고 싶어요

그렇게 큰 이불을 어떻게 짓냐고요

조그만 손으로 커다란 손주 이불 만지는 할머니 생각이 나서요

큰 할머니 삼신 할미의 사랑 생각이 나서요

받기만 한 사랑을 줄 때가 된 것 같아서요

I would love to tuck the Earth into a massive cotton-wool duvet

Are you asking how on earth I am going to make it?

Well, it's a thought that came from a granny's tiny hands

which makes a grandkid's big duvet

It's a thought that came from *Samshin Granny*'s love who oversees the birth of a child

It seems that the time to reciprocate the love that I received has come

I turned into an egg

I became a tiny egg

I am a skinny egg without freshness

After suffering from unbearable pain, after dropping my cheeks and drops of

clotted blood, I have now turned into a tiny egg

I have become a naïve egg which contains only love

Since I don't know anything but you, I took off all my clothes and became an egg

알이 되었어요

작은 알 되었어요

아무런 살 붙잖은 앙상한 알 되었어요

사랑 땜에 끙끙 앓다 따귀 빼고 선지 뺀 작은 알 되었어요

사랑으로만 똘똘 뭉친 철없는 알 되었어요

당신 말고는 암것도 몰라 걸친 옷 모두 벗고 알되고 말았어요

검은 구름

Coal-black Cloud

하늘 가득 검은 구름 몰려왔어

어쩔 수 없는 일도 있는 법이야

하악하악

눈감고 주저앉으려 했어

그때 당신이 오셨지

구름 낀 이마 위로 후둑후둑 빗물 떨어지고 맑은 하늘 다락같이 열리더군

그때 사랑이 오셨지

Pitch black clouds have thronged together and filled the whole sky

There are some things that can be undone

Howl Bawl

I was about to collapse, my eyes closing

Then you appeared

Rain started to drip onto my cloud-shaded forehead and the clear sky opened up

just like an attic

That's when love landed on me

나는 네가 좋아서 순한 양이 되었지

풀밭 같은 너의 가슴에 내 마음은 뛰어 놀았지

이제 꿈을 꾸어야겠구나

오늘 밤 꿈에는 내가 풀밭이 되련다 너는 순한 양이 되려므나

잊지 못할 나의 꿈 나의 사랑아

In adoring you I became a gentle lamb

I romped around in your heart –just like a lamb in a green field

Now it is time to dream

In my dream tonight, I shall become the green field so as to let you be the gentle lamb

Oh my unforgettable dream, my love

If I ever can be spared to be reborn, it will be all for you

Just like a bucket from a well waits in that deep well whilst weeping bitterly,

I can't stop thinking of you

Can I be reborn?

If I can, it will be only for you, only because you are waiting for me

in the deep well of this life

다시 태어날 수 있다면 오로지 당신 때문일 거예요

깊은 우물 속에서 목놓아 기다리는 두레박처럼 당신이 자꾸만 떠오르거든요

그럴 수 있을까요

다시 태어날 수 있다면 오로지 이생의 우물 깊은 곳에서 날 기다리는

당신 때문일 거예요

공 하나 내게로 날아왔어요

얼결에 한가득 가슴에 안았어요

그때 난생 처음 당신 모습 보았어요

난생 처음 사랑을 안았어요

지금도 그때처럼 한가득 안고 있어요

아직도 거기서 날 보고 계신 당신 때문에 한가득 그 사랑 놓을 수 없어요

A ball flew over to me

I grasped it to myself on an impulse

That's when I saw you for the first time

That's when I first embraced love

I am still embracing it in full, just like that moment

I can't let go of this full-filled love as you are still standing there, looking at me

Thirst began with you but it all ended through you

Yesterday, you were a fleeting moment which vanishes through one's fingers

But now, you are an eternity which comes back through a thousand hands

You are a murmuring stream inside of me

I shall not hold on to you anymore

당신으로 하여 목마름을 시작하였으나 당신으로 하여 목마름을 끝하였어요
어제 당신은 손가락 사이로 사라지는 찰나였으나
이제 당신은 천 개의 손으로 돌아오는 영원이에요
내 안의 시냇물 되어 졸졸 흐르는 당신
더 이상 당신을 잡지 않아요

한숨이 나왔어

얼굴이 말이 아니더라구

파란 이끼가 끼었더라니까

손바닥으로 얼굴을 쓰다듬어 주었어

하는 수 없이 꽃필 때마다 모아둔 꿀 한 국자 입에 넣어주었어

아껴둔 거지만 얼굴이 말이 아니더라구

빈 꿀단지 들여다보다 웃음이 나왔어

I heaved a sigh

He looked dreadful

There was even some green moss on him

I stroked his face tenderly

I couldn't help but feed him a spoonful of honey

Such precious honey I had saved whenever flowers bloomed

It had to be used up, because his face was so awful

Looking into the empty honey jar, I started to laugh

아네모네 한송이 바람에 흩어져요

바람이 낳았다가 바람이 거두어요

바람 때문에 눈물도 흩어져요

바람에 실려 문득 사라지는 것 그런 게 사랑인가요

아네모네 그대 얼굴 눈동자에 새겼어요

바람 불어도 그대 꽃얼굴 사라지지 않아요

An Anemone scatters in the wind

Born by the wind and ended by the wind

Tears scatter in the wind too

Is this sudden vanishing upon the wind meant to be love?

The Anemone is engraved on your eyes

Even as the wind rises, my darling, your flowery face will not vanish

쓴바귀처럼 입맛 쓴 짝사랑을 맛본 적 있나요

가장 숭고한 사랑은 짝사랑이에요

짝사랑이 없었다면 세상은 버얼써 망했을 거예요

인류는 진즉에 멸망했을 거라구요

제가 무슨 말을 하는지 당신은 모르실 거예요

당신은 아무것도 몰라요

Have you ever had a crush on someone which felt as bitter as an Ixeris?

The most noble kind of love must be an unrequited love

If there was no such crush, the world must have ended a long time ago

Mankind must have fallen eons ago

You won't fathom what I am saying

You know nothing

별처럼 빛나는 사랑을 할래요

밤새워 호올로 빛나다가 눈 비비며 일어난 당신 앞에 홀연히 반짝일래요

별처럼 맑은 눈 크게 떴다가 게슴츠레 잠 속으로 돌아가는

그리운 당신 모습 지켜볼래요

동트는 새벽까지 사랑의 파수꾼이 될래요

Twinkling love-like the stars is what I am going to have

After shining all alone through the night,

I shall sparkle before you as you get up and rub your eyes

I shall keep an eye on you - who I so longed for – while you open your eyes wide

and drift away again

I shall become your love guardian until dawn

검은 구름
Coal-black Cloud
4-10

We become speechless when we see white snow

Words disappear and exclamations come out

Wow or Ah – you were that kind of person, a person who does not need words

I then became silent

Love of which makes words needless

I have learnt that kind of love from you

하얀 눈을 보면 숨이 멎잖아요

말이 사라지고 탄식이 나오잖아요

와아 아니면 아아 당신은 그런 분이었어요 말이 필요없는 사람

저도 갈수록 말이 없어졌어요

말이 필요없는 사랑

당신을 만나 그런 사랑 알았어요

어디선가 날 부르는 당신 소리 들려요

가만히 귀 기울여 당신 소리 들어요

하던 일 내려놓고 당신께 달려가요

한아름 꽃바구니 가슴에 품었어요

강아지도 멍멍멍 날 따라 달려가요

멀리 계신 당신께 큰 소리로 말해요

기다려요 곧 갈께요

I hear you calling out to me from somewhere

I hold still and listen to you

I put down my work and rush to you

An armful of flowers are in my bosom

Woof woof, a puppy is following me too

I call out aloud to the place faraway, where you are

Wait for me, I am coming

황금빛 지렁이

A Golden Earthworm

Waiting is not over yet

It will be over when the five-coloured clouds drift into the sky

But I don't know when that would be

If only I knew, I could let my heart out and be laid down peacefully

If only I knew, I could be laid down as a golden earthworm and keep an eye

on the alley where you will be returning to

아직 기다려야 한다네

하늘에 오색 구름 날리면 때가 온 거라네

하지만 그게 언제일지 알 수 없다네

그걸 안다면 팔딱이는 심장 내어놓고 조용히 쉬일 수 있으련만

땅에 황금빛 지렁이로 누워 네가 돌아오는 길목을 지킬 수 있으련만

Did you say that it has been a long time since we last met?

Oh, you remember me from my old days

You said that I was as pretty as a newly blossomed flowery star

A-ha! It was you, the young wolf, running across the summer field

Perhaps we were one once

Still, I can't figure out who you are

The old memory of love is so luminous

오랜만이라고 하셨나요
오래전 제 모습을 기억하신다구요
갓 피어난 별꽃처럼 예뻤다구요
여름 들판을 뛰어다닌 젊은 늑대가 당신이셨군요
어쩌면 우리 하나였던 것도 같아요
여전히 누구신지 모르겠어요
옛사랑의 기억이 휘황하군요

하얀 꽃 손에 든 다정보살이 날 보고 있었어

다가가 붉은 꽃 불쑥하고 내밀었지

하얀 꽃 온데간데 없고 붉은 꽃 그녀 손에 들려 있더군

불현듯 가슴을 만져보니 가슴 복판이 뻥하니 뚫린 거야

관세음보살 사랑보살에게 내 마음 빼앗겼나봐

A warm-hearted bodhisattva with a white flower in her hand was looking at me

I went up to her and stuck out my hand to her, holding a red flower

Now the white flower is nowhere to be seen and the red flower is in her hand

I fumble for my heart but you see, there is a pop, a hole in the middle of it

My heart must have been stolen by the Avalokitesvara, and given to

the bodhisattva of love

사과처럼 부끄러워요 날 사랑하는 거 맞냐며 빨간 사과처럼 굴러다녔거든요

당신이 품어주지 않았더라면 멍들어 버려질 뻔 했으니까요

마침내 오늘이에요 상쾌한 봄비가 온몸을 적셔요

어쩐지 한숨이 나와요

맞아요 겨울이 가고 봄이 왔어요

I am as shy as an apple, which has been tumbling all over the place, like a red-

skinned apple, asking whether you actually love me

Because if you didn't pick me up and embrace me, I could have been bruised and

thrown away

Today has arrived at last and the bracing Spring rain is bedewing my whole body

Somewhere a sigh is let out

That's right, Winter is over and Spring has arrived

천사가 아파요

천사의 신음소리 멀리서 들려요

구슬픈 새소리 같아요

아득한 파도소리 같아요

세상이 슬픈 이유를 이제야 알겠어요

천사가 아픈데 세상이 기쁠 리 있겠어요

우리 손모아 기도해요

다시 기쁜 세상 위해 두손모아 기도해요

The angel is feeling poorly

Her groans reach out into the distance

It sounds like the plaintive cry of a bird

It sounds like waves from far in the distance

I now know why the world is in sorrow

How can the world be jolly or happy when the angel is feeling so poorly

Let's join hands and pray together

Let's join our two hands and pray that the world becomes a delightful place once again

천사인 줄 몰랐어요 작은 여자가 작은 소리로 말하는데요
도란도란 이야기 속에 펑하고 놀라운 세상 보이는 거예요
깜짝 놀라 자세히 보니 반짝이는 날개를 달고 있더라구요
그녀가 천사인 줄 예전엔 미처 몰랐어요

I never knew she was an angel, since she was just a little girl speaking

with her little voice

A startling world appeared with a pop from the murmuring of the gathering

As I took a closer look, oh my, there were the glittering wings

I had never known that she was an angel

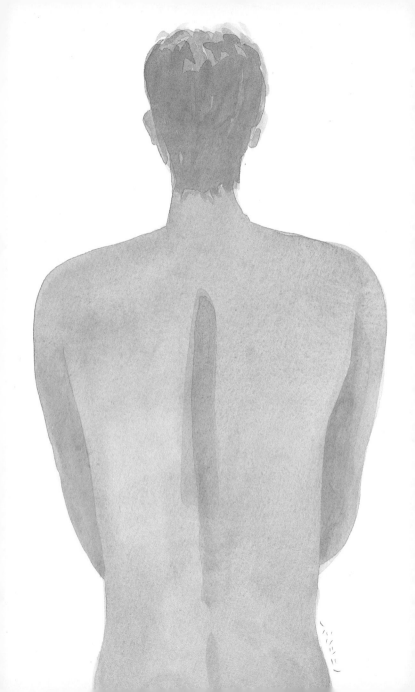

말없이 쓰다듬으며 등에게 말을 전했어

왜 그런지 모르지만 널 사랑해

말없이 흐느끼며 등이 대답했어

왜 그런지 모르지만 나도 널 사랑해 하지만 기다려 줄래 두려운 것이 많거든

어디선가 노랫소리 들려와

알아 사랑은 기다림이라는 걸 알아

Without uttering a single word, I stroke the flying lantern

"I don't know why but I love you."

The flying lantern answered back in sobs

"Same here. But will you please bear with me because I am dead scared?"

I hear the sound of singing from somewhere

I know love is all about waiting

봄새 소리

Sound of Spring Birdsong

My hands reach up to the mint-green sky where the Spring birdsong comes from

I am going on to my tippy toes so that I can catch it,

even though I only saw it in my dreams

My hands are stained with the fresh green

Oh dear, I can't get rid of the colour

There is no way I can go back to having unstained hands again

I can never go back to the loveless world

봄새 소리 들리는 연록의 하늘이 손에 닿아요
꿈에 본 하늘이지만 까치발로 잡을래요
신록의 물감이 손바닥에 묻어나요
에그머니 물감이 지워지지 않네요
다시는 흰손으로 돌아갈 수 없어요
사랑 없는 나라로 다시는 가지 않아요

사랑은 단칼에 고백해야 한다는데

뭐라고 해야 할까

차라리 아무 말도 못하고 묵묵히 돌아서는데

뒷전에 서 있던 속마음이 불쑥 나섰어 내가 말해볼까

하얀 속마음이 아름다워 그 마음에 내가 이끌렸어

우와 속마음이 나서는 건 생전 처음이야

It is said that a confession of love should be bold and strong

How should I confess mine?

Not knowing what to say, I turn away deflated

Just then, my hidden inner-heart suddenly piped up "Shall I try?"

I was entranced by the sheer sweetness of its purity

Oh, this is the very first time that my inner-heart has stepped forward like this

황금빛 지렁이

A Golden Earthworm

6-3

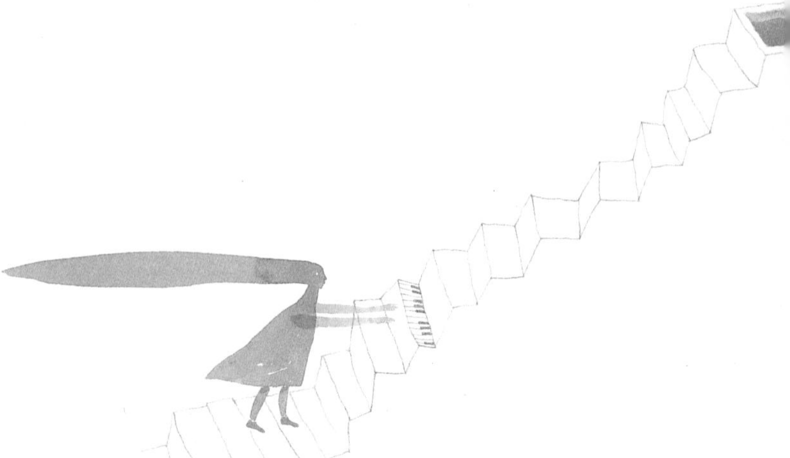

당신은 누구시길래

내 마음 가져갔나요

당신과 나 사이에 하늘 문이 있다는 걸 알아요

당신이 열고 오신 작은 문이 하늘 문이라는 걸 알아요

함께 본 하늘이 새하늘이라는 걸 알아요

당신 때문에 울고 있어요

당신 때문에 웃고 있어요

How did you manage to take my heart?

Who on earth are you?

I know there is a door-to-the-sky between us

I know the tiny door you opened to come to me is the door-to-the-sky

I know the sky we saw together is a new sky

I am crying because of you

I am laughing because of you

A big gale is blowing and a small wind follows

Whoosh, Whoosh, the big and small wind are passing by

I wonder where the world is heading to

"It's heading to the empty field."

Would that mean that a beautiful world is coming?

Following the winds, I am already standing in the empty field

큰 바람 불어요 작은 바람 따라 불어요

크고 작은 바람 우웅 우웅 지나가요 있잖아요

세상은 어디로 흘러가는 걸까요

아무것도 없는 허허벌판으로 가는 중이야

그럼 아름다운 세상이 올까요

바람따라 어느새 빈 벌판으로 왔어요

There is a speechless angel, an angel without a face

With her big flapping wings, she came down from the sky and landed in the

garden just like the white snow lands thick on the ground

Tossing and turning, I try to sleep on a winter night

As I toss and turn, I awaken and there it is, a dazzling white gift from the angel

Life can be as dazzling as this

말없는 천사가 있어요 얼굴없는 천사가 있어요

큰 날개 저으며 하늘에서 내려왔어요 하얀 눈이 쌓이듯

마당으로 내려왔어요

겨울밤 뒤척이며 잠들었다가

겨울아침 뒤척이며 깨어났더니 천사의 선물이 하얗게 눈부시네요

이처럼 아름다운 인생이에요

할머니가 말했어

The Granny Said

쿨쿨 잠자던 할머니가 번쩍 눈뜨며 말했어 트럭을 불러 이사를 하려고 했어

밑도 끝도 없는 꿈이야

내가 말했어 이사를 할 수 있다면 고치에서 나갈 수 있을 거야

나비가 될 지도 몰라

마주보며 빙그레 웃었어

밑도 끝도 없는 사랑이야

Grandma, who had fallen into a deep sleep, opened her eyes widely in a start,

and said "I called for a van to move house – such a strange and silly dream."

I said, "If we can move, we'll be able to escape this cocoon."

"Who knows, perhaps we might even turn into butterflies."

We smiled at each other

What a strange and silly kind of love

안개 자욱한 지평선 너머로 새하늘 새땅이 와요

나도 새사람 되어 그곳으로 가요

당신이 그 나라 세우신 걸 알아요

삽질 수만 번 가래질 수억만 번 마침내 세워진 기적의 나라

눈물 없이는 살아갈 수 없는 기쁨의 나라 아닌가요

A new sky and a new land are appearing beyond the brumous horizon

I, too, am becoming a new person, and will depart for that place

I know you built this country

A miraculous country which is finally built after spades and shovels have

struck the earth millions of times

Isn't it a delightful country that no one can't settle there, not without tears?

깊은 밤 대청마루에 키큰 나비 날아왔어

반가운 마음에 나비 등에 업혔어 대문 위에 환한 등불 걸어두고

사랑의 시작을 알렸어

가물한 새벽 대문마다 오색 등불 걸리고 인파 넘치는 거리에

사랑이 선포되는 걸 보았어 나비 등에 업혀서 보았어

In the dead of night, a tall butterfly flew into the wooden porch

So pleased was I that I rode on her back and announced the beginning of

love with a brightly lit lamp hanging on the front gate

With the five-coloured lamps hanging on each gate in the blurry dawn,

I heard the announcement of love from the street flooding with people

while I was riding on her back

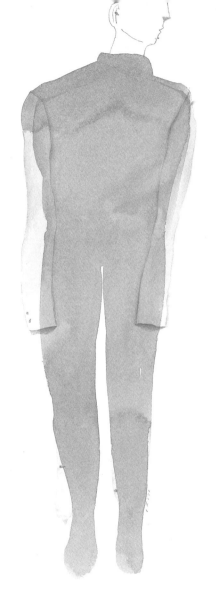

어머니가 말했어 어젯밤 꿈에 자네 옷을 지었어

포목전 주인이 아끼는 귀한 천을 비나리로 얻어다 은장도 바늘로

눈물눈물 지었어

어머니께 말했어 사랑으로 지은 옷을 주셨으니 사랑으로 지은

무엇을 드릴까요

어머니가 웃었어 자꾸만 웃었어

Mum said, "My dear, I made your dress in my dream last night"

"With the draper's most beloved fabric that I had begged him for,

I shed my tears with every single stitch with an ornamental silver needle."

I asked her "For the dress that you have made with love,

with what made from my love shall I repay?"

Mum laughed over and over again

꽃신 한 켤레

A Pair of Flowery Shoes

수만 개 바늘 깔린 험한 산길을 맨발로 걸어온 기막힌 생애

바늘길 굽이에서 마주친 꽃신 한 켤레

서둘러 발에 신고 일어서니 수만 장 꽃잎이 축복처럼 떨어져요

이제는 꽃신 신고 걸어갈 기막힌 생애입니다

An exorbitant life of barefooted walking on a steep mountain path

which is covered by millions of needles

I bump into a pair of flowery shoes as I turn around this needle strewn path

As I put them on in a hurry and get up, millions of petals fall down as a blessing

A breath-taking life with these flowery shoes is now upon me

하늘에서 비가 내려요

하늘이 엄청 슬픈가 봐요

토닥토닥 위로하고 싶지만 하늘의 등이 어딘지 알 수가 없어서요

궁리 끝에 두손 모아 기도했어요

하늘님 하늘님 울지 마세요

하늘이 엉엉 울기 시작했어요

제가 하늘을 달랜 거 맞나 봐요

Rain is falling down from the sky

The sky must be so upset

I wish I could give a tap on his back but I don't know where his back is

After racking my brain, I joined my hands and prayed

Dear Sky, dear Sky, please do not cry

The sky started to burst into tears

I must have managed to comfort him

볼수록 예뻐요 이렇게 예쁠 수 없어요

어색한 음치의 노래 갈수록 커지는 슬픔 그렇게 사랑인 줄 진작에 알아요

봄이 오면 산에 들에 노래가 피거든요

꽃들처럼 나투어 노래가 피거든요

제 눈에 피어나는 붉은 노래 보이시죠

So pretty, the more I see it, the prettier it gets

I have long known that love is like a growing sorrow on the rising singing of

the awkwardly tone-deaf

I know because singing blooms in the mountains and fields

when Spring arrives

I know because singing blooms, just as the flowers do one after the other

Surely you can see the scarlet song blooming from my eyes?

아름다운 공작새가 나의 정원으로 날아왔어

견딜 수 없는 마음으로 공작새를 바라보았어

어째서 당신이라고 믿었을까

아름다운 당신이 나의 정원으로 날아왔어

조용히 숨을 멈추고 아름다움을 바라보았어

오직 아름다움이 우리를 구원할 거예요

A gorgeous peacock flew into my garden

I looked at the peacock with an unbearable heart

Why on earth did I believe it was you?

My beautiful darling, you flew into my garden

My breathing paused, I admired your beauty in silence

Only 'beauty' will save us.

어디 갔다 이제 왔니

얼마나 기다렸는데 기다리다 코가 비뚤어질 뻔했는데

큰 일이 난 줄 알았잖니

정말 다행이구나

그냥 고맙다는 말이면 될 것 같구나 그냥 다행이라는 말이면 될 것 같구나

사랑한다는 말일랑 가슴에 묻어도 될 것 같구나

Where have you been?

I have been waiting for ages and my nose was about to get bent out of shape

I thought something serious had happened

Phew, I am glad you're okay

A simple 'Thank you' would be enough, a simple 'What a relief'

would be enough

For now, 'I love you' would be fine to be buried in my heart

A hand came to me

"I do love you, it's an exquisite love" the hand said

Feeling the wetness in my eyes, I drifted away

There I was standing by a lake in my dream

I put the starry light floating on the surface of the water into my hands

Tilting the now starry hands, I was dry-washing my face

Goodness gracious! Two morning stars have gone in my eyes

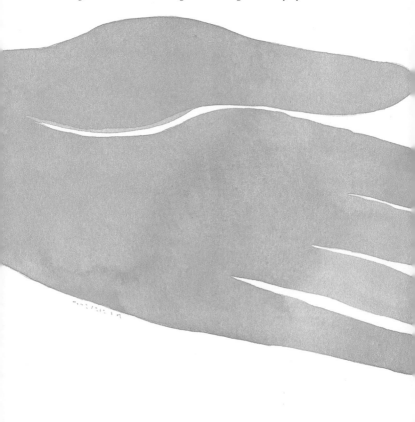

손이 내게로 왔어요
널 사랑해 아름다운 사랑이야 손이 말했어요
눈가에 물기를 느끼며 까무룩 잠들었어요
꿈 속에서 호수가에 갔어요
수면 위의 별빛을 손에 넣었어요
별빛 손 기울여 마른 세수 하다가
어이쿠 샛별 두 개 눈에 넣었어요

빨강 장미 한송이 그대 발치에 드려요

진한 꽃잎이 피처럼 붉어요

길고 긴 세월의 터널에서 이제야 나왔어요

나와보니 벌써 해가 지네요

저녁 노을 아래 사무치는 꽃 한송이 그대 발치에 드려요

해는 져도 사랑은 지지 않아요

Here I present to you a single red rose and place it on your feet

The rich petal is as red as blood

I am finally out from the tunnel after years and years

I am out but the Sun is sinking

Here I present to you a single red rose, inked under the sunset,

and place it on your feet

Love never sinks even though the Sun does

하늘이 다른 몸 주시어

그 몸에 당신 품이 허락되지 않는다면 아무리 아름다운 몸이어도

탐내지 않을래요

서산에 해 떨어져 가진 몸 벗어놓고 갈 때 당신 품이 허락하신

아름다운 시간 떠올리며 작은 몸 개어놓고 갈래요

Even Heaven allows me a different body

If it doesn't let me be in your arms I wouldn't lust for it,

no matter how stunning it might be

When I have to take off this body and leave, following the sundown in

the western mountain, I shall recall the beautiful time your bosom

allowed me in, as I fold up this small body and leave it behind

긴 얼굴을 가진 슬픈 사람을 만났어

눈두덩에도 눈매에도 덕지덕지 슬픔이 묻어 있었어

차마 고개를 돌리려는데 불쑥 그이의 눈동자가 보이는 거야

칠흙 같은 눈동자 속에 뒤집혀진 배 한 척 있는 거야

긴 얼굴을 가슴에 묻고 말았어

I met a sad person with a long face

I was about to turn away from him since the sadness was stained

everywhere around his eyes, even on their outer edges

But then his eyes struck me all of a sudden

There was an upside-down boat in their inky darkness

I had to bury that long face into my heart

오늘이에요 꼭 와야 할 그날이에요

자꾸만 손을 씻으며 마음을 지웠거든요

혹시라도 더러운 맘

그날을 막을까 해서요

무슨 날이냐구요

이젠 그것조차 까맣게 잊었어요

손을 씻다가 마음도 지워졌나 봐요

참 기쁜 날이라는 것 그것만 알아요

It is today, the day which must come

I emptied my mind by washing my hands over and over again, because

I was afraid that my stained mind would stop the day from coming

Are you asking what day it is?

I have forgotten completely

Maybe while I was washing my hands, my mind was also washed away

I only know that this is such a joyful day

괜찮아 다시 시작하면 되잖아

지우개를 줄께

눈 꼭감고 지난 일을 지워요

칠판에 남은 어지러운 낙서 깨끗이 지워요

까치발로 몸 세워 남김없이 지워요

하얀 백묵 손에 들고 나무처럼 팔 벌려

흔들리는 사랑의 말

다시 시작해야 하잖아

No worries, it can be started again

Here is an eraser

Close your eyes and wipe out the past

Getting on your tippy-toes, clean up all the messy scribblings

on the chalk board

We all know that we have to start the quivering words of love again

by holding a piece of chalk and opening up our arms like a tree

행복은 자취를 감추었고

Happiness has Vanished

Happiness vanished from this world so long ago and the

world is now full of despair

There is a saying

When one tries to climb the cliff of despair

When one so desperately tries to grasp hold of anything

A tiny, poisonous plant grows forth from the tip of one's finger

It's called happiness.

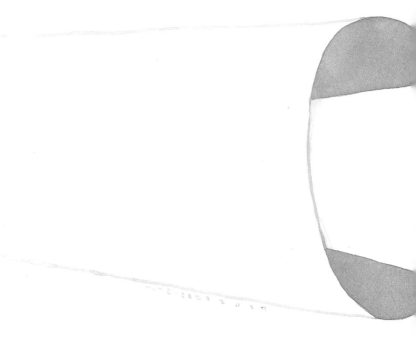

행복은 오래 전 세상에서 자취를 감추었고 세상은 오직 절망으로 가득해요
하지만 절망의 끝에서
낭떠러지를 건너기 위해 필사적으로 무언가를 잡으려 할 때
손가락 끝에서 독이 든 작은 식물이 자란다네요
이 작은 식물을 행복이라 부른다지요

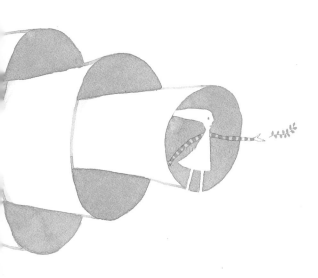

너에게 하고 싶은 말이 많은데 입가에서 뱅뱅 맴도는데

나도 따라 입 속으로 들어가 버렸는데

이렇게 끝날 수는 없는데

에에취 재채기가 나오면서

나도 따라 입 밖으로 튀어나왔어

다시 시작해도 되겠지 너에게 해주고 싶은 말이 정말 많거든

So many words for you are teetering on my lips

I too am swallowed back into my own mouth

It can't end like this

Achoo! A sneeze brings me out

Now I can start again, right?

Because there are so many words waiting for you.

당신에게 얼마나 큰 사랑이 있는지 알아요

당신은 오매불망 사랑 생각만 한다는 걸 알아요

사랑 생각에 사랑 따위 잊은 것도 알아요

어처구니 없는 당신 사랑에 안기고 싶어요

눈물이 나요 그런 사랑 없을 줄 알았는데 쾅쾅 눈물이 나요

I know how enormous your love is

I know that you think of nothing but love all the time whether walking or

sleeping

I know that you even forget love, thinking of love

I want to throw myself into your absurd love

Tears fall, I didn't imagine such a love, big tear drops fall

When you miss me, please have a plate of spring salad

Please put a thought of me into that bitter taste, and please pick a thought

of me from that hazy scent

If we are not filled with the memory of love, somewhat like a spring scent,

you and I, we are nothing.

제 생각 나면 봄나물 한접시 맛나게 잡수어요

알싸한 나물 맛에 제 생각 놓으시고 아릿한 향기에 제 생각 집으세요

봄향기 닮은 사랑의 기억으로 과양 채워지지 않으면

당신과 나, 우리는 아무것도 아니어요

큰 비가 와요
큰 물이 하늘 호수에서 쏟아져요 모두들 몸을 씻을 시간이에요
묵은 때 벗을 시간이에요
쏟아지는 비에 몸을 맡기면 잊혀진 사랑의 시간이 와요
정갈한 몸이 되어 서로들 몸을 섞을 시간이 와요

Heavy rain pours down

Big rain drops fall from the lake in the sky

Everybody, it's time to take a shower, time to rub off the old dirt

Entrusting ourselves to the heavy rain, the time of forgotten love approaches

The time when we merge our pure bodies together arrives.

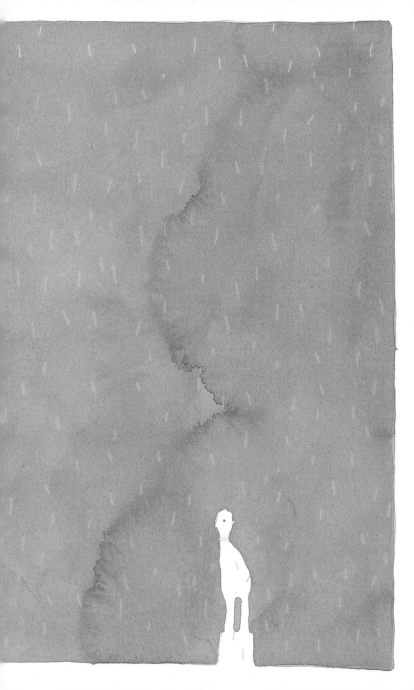

산타 할아버지가 빨강 모자 쓰고 굴뚝으로 들어와요

굴뚝 밑에 양말 한짝 걸어두고 쿨쿨 잠들어요

평생 기다렸지만 할아버지는 오지 않았어요

더 이상 참을 수 없어요 집집마다 다니며 양말 속에 선물을 넣을 거예요

할아버지가 오지 않았잖아요

Father Christmas with his red hat comes into the chimney

I fall asleep, hanging a stocking under the chimney

I have been waiting for him my whole life, but in vain

I can't bear it anymore

I will visit every single house and leave a present in the stockings

Because he didn't come

슬픈 아이

A Child in Sorrow

I have to look after a child, a child in sorrow

Where has all his joy disappeared to?

Oh, I found it

But it is sunshine, hands of the warm sun, a thousand hands

Holding one hand among them, then I put it on his sorrow

The smiling child is the Sun

아이를 돌보아야 해요 슬픈 아이에요

아이의 기쁨은 어디로 사라진 걸까요

앗 찾았어요

하지만 그건 햇살이네요 따사로운 햇님의 손들이네요

천개의 손들이네요 손 하나 잡아 아이의 슬픔 위에 올려 놓아요

빙그레 웃는 아이가 햇님이에요

나무는 모든 것을 알아요

모든 것을 아는 나무가 말해요 혼자서 슬프면 영원히 슬프다구요

비로소 모든 것을 알아요 둘이서 슬프면 슬프지 않을 것을 알아요

이제 나무에게로 가요 나무와 몸을 섞고 영원한 기쁨이 되어요.

A tree knows everything

The know-it-all tree is saying, "If you are sad alone, you shall be sad forever"

I finally understand everything, that if two of us are sad together then

we shall not be sad

Now I reach to the tree, blending myself with it and turn into an eternal joy

Gazing at your feet makes my tears drop again and again

They've been enduring a whole life of carrying you

You've been living in comfort on high, but they've been suffering

in theirlowly position

Please let me have your feet, I will wash them, wash away the lowly past

with my tears

당신의 발 눈에 넣으면 자꾸만 눈물이 나요

당신의 몸 이고지고 한세상 견뎠잖아요

당신이야 높은 곳에서 편안히 지나셨지만 발이야 낮은 곳에서

어렵사리 견뎠잖아요

당신의 발 제게 주세요 지나간 낮은 세월 눈물로 씻어드릴게요.

바람을 만났어요

바람과 둘이서 사랑에 빠졌어요

바람처럼 짧았지만 틀림없이 그랬어요

다정한 소리로 바람이 속삭였어요 우리 만나서 참 다행이야

바람은 휘잉 가버렸지만 아직도 그곳에 있어요

꼼짝않고 거기 못박혀 있어요

I encountered the wind

I fell in love with it

It was as fleeting as the wind itself, but surely happened

The wind whispered with a gentle voice, "We are so lucky to meet each other"

Whoosh, the wind has disappeared, but I am still there

I am nailed there, unable to move

당신이 말했어 얼굴을 봉숭아꽃처럼 물들이며 봉숭아씨 터뜨리듯

느닷없이 말했어 아무래도 그대와 난 어울리지 않나봐

도무지 그대처럼 속마음 드러낼 수 없거든

내가 말했어 당신 얼굴 한가득 봉숭아씨 붙어 있잖아

대박 수다쟁이 얼굴이잖아

You uttered abruptly with your face blushing like a balsam flower,

like balsam seeds are popping, "I don't think we are well-suited,

as I can't reveal my inner heart like you do"

I said "Look at your face, fully covered with those balsam seeds.

That's the face of a real chatterbox"

두꺼비 신랑이랑 백년가약을 맺었어요

하필이면 그런 짝이냐고요

두꺼비가 어때서요

갸우뚱 고개를 저으시는군요

그래요 뜬금없는 사랑이 최고의 사랑이라고요

가진 거라곤 덩어리 맘뿐인

두꺼비 사랑이 얼마나 복덩어리인지 잘 아시면서 그래요

I made a hundred-year-marriage-vow with a toad groom

Are you asking how on earth such a match was made?

What's wrong with a toad?

You are still tilting your head in doubt

Yes that's right, an unexpected love is the best kind of love

What a blessing the toad's love is who is nothing but big-hearted

You already know this anyway